Note to parents, carers and teachers

Read it yourself is a series of modern stories, favourite characters and traditional tales written in a simple way for children who are learning to read. The books can be read independently or as part of a guided reading session.

Each book is carefully structured to include many high-frequency words vital for first reading. The sentences on each page are supported closely by pictures to help with understanding, and to offer lively details to talk about.

The books are graded into four levels that progressively introduce wider vocabulary and longer stories as a reader's ability and confidence grows.

Ideas for use

- Begin by looking through the book and talking about the pictures. Has your child heard this story before?

- Help your child with any words he does not know, either by helping him to sound them out or supplying them yourself.

- Developing readers can be concentrating so hard on the words that they sometimes don't fully grasp the meaning of what they're reading. Answering the puzzle questions at the end of the book will help with understanding.

For more information and advice on Read it yourself and book banding, visit www.ladybird.com/readityourself

Book Band 5

Level 1 is ideal for children who have received some initial reading instruction. Each story is told very simply, using a small number of frequently repeated words.

Special features:

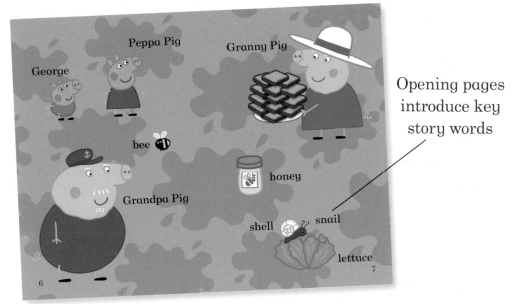

Opening pages introduce key story words

Careful match between story and pictures

Large, clear type

Educational Consultant: Geraldine Taylor
Book Banding Consultant: Kate Ruttle

LADYBIRD BOOKS

UK | USA | Canada | Ireland | Australia
India | New Zealand | South Africa

Ladybird Books is part of the Penguin Random House group of companies
whose addresses can be found at global.penguinrandomhouse.com.

www.penguin.co.uk   www.puffin.co.uk   www.ladybird.co.uk

Text adapted from Tiny Creatures, first published by Ladybird Books, 2008
This version first published by Ladybird Books, 2013
017

Illustrations copyright © ABD Ltd/Ent. One UK Ltd, 2003
Text copyright © ABD Ltd/Ent. One UK Ltd, 2013. All rights reserved

This book is based on the
TV Series 'Peppa Pig'
'Peppa Pig' is created by
Neville Astley and Mark Baker
Peppa Pig © Astley Baker Davies Ltd/
Entertainment One UK Ltd, 2003

www.peppapig.com

Printed in China

A CIP catalogue record for this book is
available from the British Library

ISBN: 978-0-723-27287-8

Little Creatures

Written by Lorraine Horsley

George

Peppa Pig

bee

Grandpa Pig

Granny Pig

honey

shell snail

lettuce

This is Peppa Pig.

This is George.
George is her little brother.

This is Grandpa Pig
and this is Granny Pig.

Peppa, George and Grandpa
are in the garden.

Grandpa gives Peppa
a lettuce.

"What is that?" says Peppa.

"It is a little snail,"
says Grandpa.

George likes the snail.

"Where is the snail now, Grandpa?" says Peppa.

"It is in its shell," says
Grandpa. "The shell is the
snail's little house."

George wants to be a snail
in a little house.

"I want to be a snail in a little house, too!" says Peppa. "Grandpa, we will eat your lettuce!"

Now Peppa and George's
friends are in the
garden, too.

Buzz! Buzz! Buzz!

"What is that?" they say.

21

"Some bees," says Grandpa.

"Where are they going?" says Peppa.

"They will be going to make some honey," says Grandpa.

"I like honey!" says Peppa.

The friends want to be bees.

"Buzz! Buzz! Buzz!"
they say.

Granny Pig is in the garden.
Granny gives Peppa and her
friends some honey to eat.

"I like bees," says Peppa.

"We like bees, too," say Peppa's friends. "We like to eat the honey they make!"

How much do you remember about Peppa Pig: Little Creatures? Answer these questions and find out!

- **What does Grandpa Pig give Peppa?**

- **Who likes the snail?**

- **Where are the bees going?**

- **What does Granny Pig give Peppa and her friends to eat?**

Look at the pictures from the story and say the order they should go in.

A

B

C

D

Answer: C, A, D, B.

Read it yourself with Ladybird

Tick the books you've read!

For children who are ready to take their first steps in reading.

Level 1

The Enormous Turnip ☐

Fairy Friends ☐

Goldilocks and the Three Bears ☐

Little Red Hen ☐

The Magic Porridge Pot ☐

Little Creatures ☐

Recycling Fun! ☐

The Princess and the Pea ☐

Cinderella ☐

Rex the Big Dinosaur ☐

The Tale of Peter Rabbit ☐

The Three Billy Goats Gruff ☐

Why Giraffe has a Long Neck ☐

Topsy and Tim Go to the Zoo ☐

The Ugly Duckling ☐

The Emperor's New Clothes ☐

For beginner readers who can read short, simple sentences with help.

Level 2

Beauty and the Beast ☐

Chicken Licken ☐

Little Red Riding Hood ☐

Nature Trail ☐

Sports Day ☐

Pirate School ☐

Rumpelstiltskin ☐

Sleeping Beauty ☐

The Gingerbread Man ☐

Sly Fox and Red Hen ☐

The Tale of Jemima Puddle-Duck ☐

The Three Little Pigs ☐

Why Lion Roarrrs! ☐

Topsy and Tim The Big Race ☐

Town Mouse and Country Mouse ☐

Dom's Dragon ☐

Available on the App Store

The Read it yourself with Ladybird app is now available for iPad, iPhone and iPod touch

App also available on Android devices